3 4028 07055 5819
HARRIS COUNTY PUBLIC LIBRARY

W9-AKC-465

To all our little rats

First published in France under the title *Le rat m'a dit . . .*

First published in the United States, Great Britain, Canada, Australia, and New Zealand in 2009 by North-South Books Inc., an imprint of NordSüd Verlag AG, Zürich, Switzerland.
Distributed in the United States by North-South Books Inc., New York.

Library of Congress Cataloging-in-Publication Data is available.
ISBN: 978-0-7358-2220-7 (trade edition)
10 9 8 7 6 5 4 3 2 1
Printed in China

www.northsouth.com

What the Rat Told Me

A Legend of the Chinese Zodiac

Marie Sellier

Catherine Louis

Wang Fei

NorthSouth
New York / London

I am going to tell you the story
of the twelve animals of the Chinese zodiac.
This story is true, I am sure,
because I heard it from the rat,
who was there.

Here is what the rat told me. . . .

One day,
at the dawn of the dawn of the world,
so long ago
that everyone has forgotten when,
the Great Emperor of Heaven
invited all the animals in creation
to visit him.
"Come, all of you," he told them.
"I will wait for you before sunrise
at the top of the Jade Mountain."

"Before sunrise!" The cat sighed and yawned.
"That is much too early for me!
I will never wake up in time."
"Don't worry," the rat told her. "Sleep peacefully.
I will wake you, and we will go together."
You must know that, in those times,
the cat and the rat were the best friends in the world.

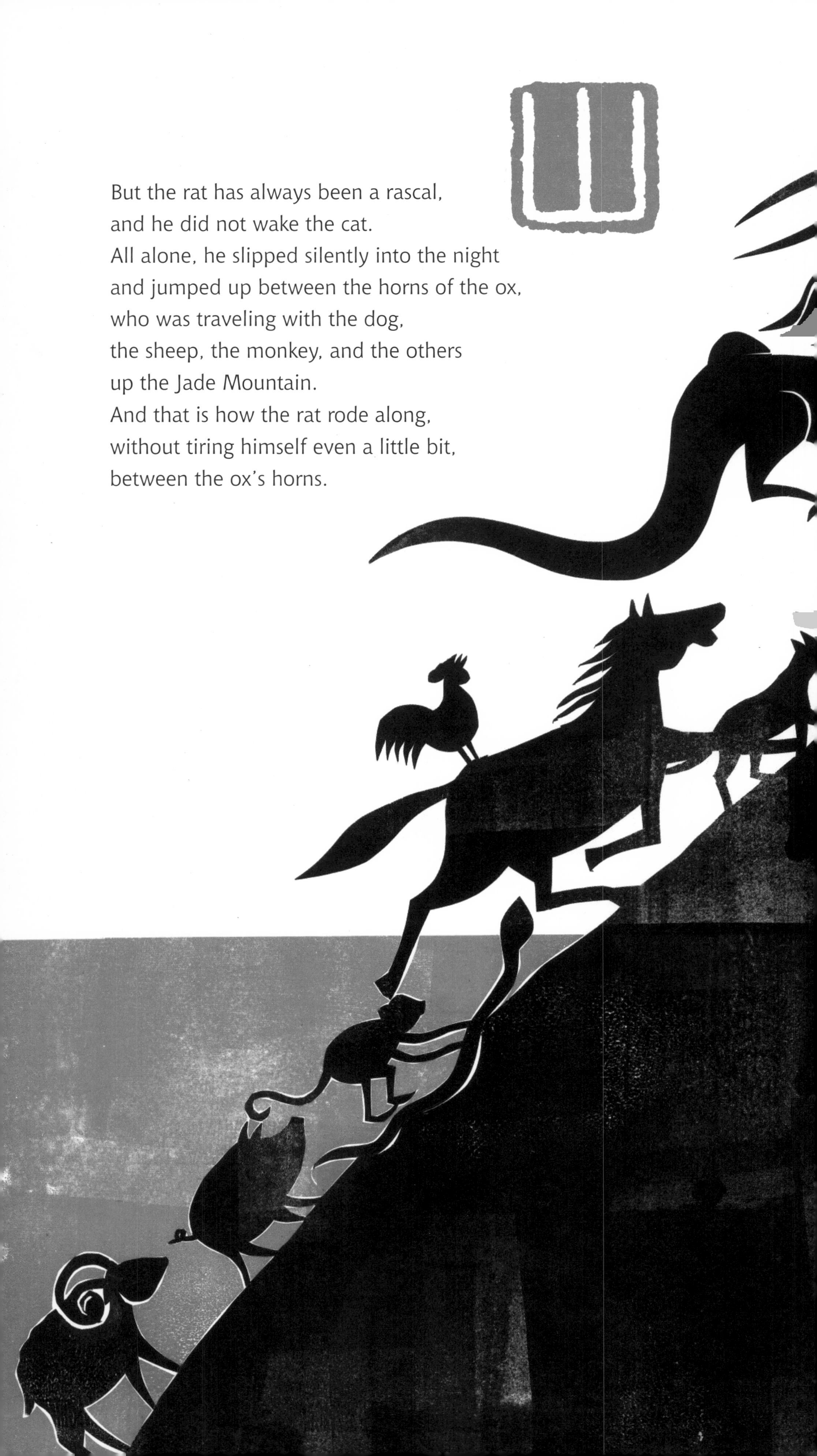

But the rat has always been a rascal,
and he did not wake the cat.
All alone, he slipped silently into the night
and jumped up between the horns of the ox,
who was traveling with the dog,
the sheep, the monkey, and the others
up the Jade Mountain.
And that is how the rat rode along,
without tiring himself even a little bit,
between the ox's horns.

鼠 "I am first!" cried the ox,
who led the procession.
But when the ox reached the top of the Jade Mountain,
the rat, in a single bound, leaped right over his head,
and landed at the feet of the Great Emperor of Heaven.
"Heavenly Majesty, here I am!" the rat exclaimed.
The Great Emperor of Heaven smiled.
"You please me, rat of the morning,
because, although little, you are lively and cunning.
I will give you the first year for all of time."
"A thousand thank-yous, Your Majesty," squeaked the rat proudly.

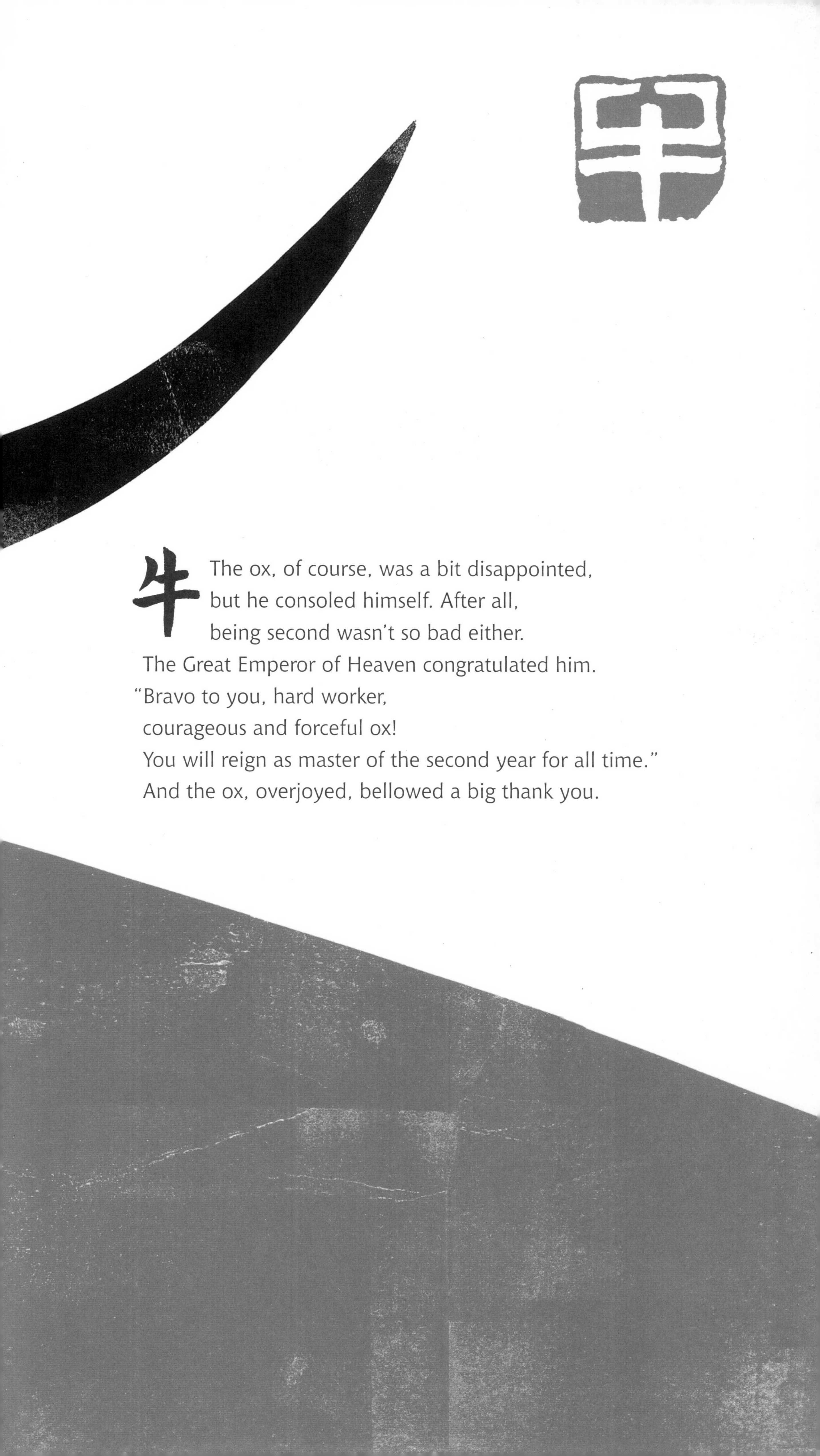

牛 The ox, of course, was a bit disappointed,
but he consoled himself. After all,
being second wasn't so bad either.
The Great Emperor of Heaven congratulated him.
"Bravo to you, hard worker,
courageous and forceful ox!
You will reign as master of the second year for all time."
And the ox, overjoyed, bellowed a big thank you.

虎 The tiger came next, and he was not happy.
What? He, the all-powerful lord of the hunt,
the charming, the sensitive, only third?
But then the Great Emperor of Heaven spoke:
"O king of the mountain, splendid tiger,
I salute your courage and your strength."
The tiger was so flattered that he forgot his disappointment
and agreed with a soft mew of thanks
to rule over the third year for all time.

兔 Fourth came a charming rabbit,
who felt so happy to come *after* the tiger,
he twitched his big ears in the wind.
"Good rabbit," said the Great Emperor of Heaven,
"you who are so supple and swift,
I want you always to be happy.
I offer you year number four for all time."
And the rabbit wiggled his little white tail
to show his pleasure.

龍 Then came the marvelous dragon,
who waited, rolling his huge eyes.
The Great Emperor of Heaven greeted him:
"Welcome to you, king of the oceans.
I know how great is your heart.
Accept the fifth year for all time,
so that all may live free and secure
under your reign.
And the happy dragon showed his thanks
by whipping the air with his long tail.

蛇 Next came the snake,
who had taken his time
and only sneaked into line
at the last moment.
"The sixth year is yours,"
the Great Emperor of Heaven told him,
"so that at last a time of wisdom may come."
The snake hissed modestly,
but it was obvious by the way he wriggled
at the emperor's feet
that he was enchanted.

馬 The horse was so impatient
to see his turn finally arrive
that he almost stepped on the snake.
"Easy, you who are always moving!"
said the Great Emperor of Heaven, laughing.
"To you, I offer the seventh year,
for your spirit of adventure,
for better or worse."
And the horse neighed with pleasure.

羊 The sheep, who had waited patiently,
now gently wiggled her ears.
"This eighth year I willingly give to you,
happy sheep, for I hold your friendship dear,"
said the Great Emperor of Heaven.
"You will reign in peace, love, and beauty."
And the grateful sheep bleated her joy.

猴 The monkey did three pirouettes
and greeted the Great Emperor of Heaven
with his most handsome carnival grin.
"You, monkey, with such a mind of your own,
I offer you year nine for all time,"
said the Great Emperor of Heaven.
"I know how crafty you are.
You will never lack for ideas
to charm and amuse."
"Ah, yes!" said the monkey,
making little cries of joy.

鷄 "At last it is my turn," said the rooster.
"For me, year ten for all time!
I will put things in order, without fail,
for I am the champion of organization."
"As you say, so shall it be; and I am delighted,"
said the Great Emperor of Heaven.
"I wish you good luck, master cock!"
And the rooster, satisfied, gave thanks
with a loud *cock-a-doodle-do.*

Now came the dog,
who approached the Great Emperor of Heaven
and licked his hand.
"Beloved master, I await your orders."
"Faithful guardian, tireless protector,"
said the Great Emperor of Heaven,
"I entrust to you the eleventh year for all time,
for you to guard and protect faithfully."
And the dog gave a little yelp of gratitude.

豬 Last of all came the pig,
all rosy and round.
"To you who are so good,
so humble, so sincere,
I offer year twelve for all time,"
said the Great Emperor of Heaven.
"Make it go around well,
in peace and good humor."
"Just right!" replied the pig,
grunting heartily.

豬

Then the golden throne of the Great Emperor of Heaven
began to glow as the sun appeared in the heavens.
It was the dawn of the world.
The earth began to turn slowly;
and all the animals, in single file,
took their places on the great wheel of time.

Rat, ox, tiger,
rabbit, dragon, snake,
horse, sheep, monkey,
rooster, dog, pig—
all twelve stepped onto the wheel,
and today—oh, yes!—
they are still there.

As for the cat?
What became of the cat?
Well you might ask.
When he finally woke up,
he well understood
that the rat had played a trick on him.
Ever since—as you must know—
cats and rats have not been friends at all!

 **Emperor of Heaven**

 **Cat**

 **Mountain**

牛虎兔龍

Which sign are you?

Rat

January 31, 1900 – February 18, 1901
February 18, 1912 – February 5, 1913
February 5, 1924 – January 24, 1925
January 24, 1936 – February 10, 1937
February 10, 1948 – January 28, 1949
January 28, 1960 – February 14, 1961
February 16, 1972 – February 2, 1973
February 2, 1984 – February 19, 1985
February 19, 1996 – February 6, 1997
February 7, 2008 – January 25, 2009

Ox

牛

February 19, 1901 – February 7, 1902
February 6, 1913 – January 25, 1914
January 25, 1925 – February 12, 1926
February 11, 1937 - January 30, 1938
January 29, 1949 – February 16, 1950
February 15, 1961 – February 4, 1962
February 3, 1973 – January 22, 1974
February 20, 1985 – February 8, 1986
February 7, 1997 – January 27, 1998
January 26, 2009 – February 23, 2010

Tiger

February 8, 1902 – January 28, 1903
January 26, 1914 – February 13, 1915
February 13, 1926 – February 1, 1927
January 31, 1938 – February 18, 1939
February 17, 1950 – February 5, 1951
February 5, 1962 – January 24, 1963
January 23, 1974 – February 10, 1975
February 9, 1986 – February 18, 1987
January 28, 1998 – February 15, 1999
February 24, 2010 – February 2, 2011

Rabbit

兔

January 29, 1903 – February 15, 1904
February 14, 1915 – February 2, 1916
February 2, 1927 – January 22, 1928
February 19, 1939 – February 7, 1940
February 6, 1951 – January 26, 1952
January 25, 1963 – February 12, 1964
February 11, 1975 – January 30, 1976
January 19, 1987 – February 16, 1988
February 16, 1999 – February 4, 2000
February 3, 2011 – January 22, 2012

Dragon

February 16, 1904 – February 3, 1905
February 3, 1916 – January 22, 1917
January 23, 1928 – February 9, 1929
February 8, 1940 – January 26, 1941
January 27, 1952 – February 13, 1953
February 13, 1964 – February 1, 1965
January 31, 1976 – February 17, 1977
February 17, 1988 – February 5, 1989
February 5, 2000 – January 23, 2001
January 23, 2012 – February 9, 2013

Snake

February 4, 1905 – January 24, 1906
January 23, 1917 – February 10, 1918
February 10, 1929 – January 29, 1930
January 27, 1941 – February 14, 1942
February 14, 1953 – February 2, 1954
February 2, 1965 – January 20, 1966
February 18, 1977 – February 6, 1978
February 6, 1989 – January 26, 1990
January 24, 2001 – February 11, 2002
February 10, 2013 – January 30, 2014

Horse

January 25, 1906 – February 12, 1907
February 11, 1918 – January 31, 1919
January 30, 1930 – February 16, 1931
February 15, 1942 – February 4, 1943
February 3, 1954 – January 23, 1955
January 21, 1966 – February 8, 1967
February 7, 1978 – January 17, 1979
January 27, 1990 – February 14, 1991
February 12, 2002 – January 31, 2003
January 31, 2014 – February 18, 2015

Sheep

February 13, 1907 – February 1, 1908
February 1, 1919 – February 19, 1920
February 17, 1931 – February 5, 1932
February 5, 1943 – January 24, 1944
January 24, 1955 – February 11, 1956
February 9, 1967 – January 29, 1968
January 18, 1979 – February 15, 1980
February 15, 1991 – February 3, 1992
February 1, 2003 – January 21, 2004
February 19, 2015 – February 7, 2016

Monkey

February 2, 1908 – January 21, 1909
February 20, 1920 – February 7, 1921
February 6, 1932 – January 25, 1933
January 25, 1944 – February 12, 1945
February 12, 1956 – January 30, 1957
January 30, 1968 – February 16, 1969
February 16, 1980 – February 4, 1981
February 4, 1992 – January 22, 1993
January 22, 2004 – February 8, 2005
February 8, 2016 – January 27, 2017

Rooster

January 22, 1909 – February 9, 1910
February 8, 1921 – January 27, 1922
January 26, 1933 – February 13, 1934
February 13, 1945 – February 1, 1946
January 31, 1957 – February 17, 1958
February 17, 1969 – February 5, 1970
February 5, 1981 – January 24, 1982
January 23, 1993 – February 9, 1994
February 9, 2005 – January 28, 2006
January 28, 2017 – February 15, 2018

Dog

February 10, 1910 – January 29, 1911
January 28, 1922 – February 15, 1923
February 14, 1934 – February 3, 1935
February 2, 1946 – January 21, 1947
February 18, 1958 – February 7, 1959
February 6, 1970 – January 26, 1971
January 25, 1982 – February 12, 1983
February 10, 1994 – January 30, 1995
January 29, 2006 – February 17, 2007
February 16, 2018 – February 4, 2019

Pig

January 30, 1911 – February 17, 1912
February 16, 1923 – February 4, 1924
February 4, 1935 – January 23, 1936
January 22, 1947 – February 9, 1948
February 8, 1959 – January 27, 1960
January 27, 1971 – February 15, 1972
February 13, 1983 – February 1, 1984
January 31, 1995 – February 18, 1996
February 18, 2007 – February 7, 2008
February 5, 2019 – January 24, 2020